32nd America's CUP
A simple guide

VALENCIA
32ND AMERICA'S
CUP

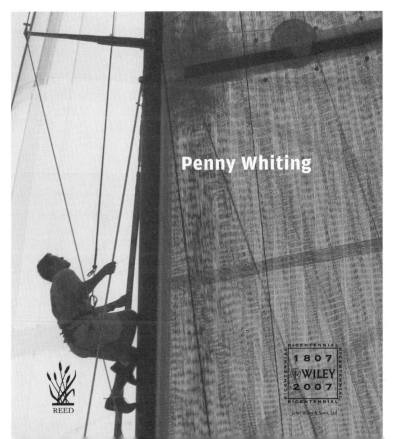

Penny Whiting

REED

1807
WILEY
2007

John Wiley & Sons, Ltd

WILEY
wiley.com

Published under licence under the Fernhurst imprint by John Wiley & Sons Ltd , The Atrium, Southern Gate, Chichester, West Sussex PO19 8SQ, England. Telephone (+44) 1243 779777. Email (orders and customer service enquiries): cs-books@wiley.co.uk. Visit our Home Page on www.wiley.com
A catalogue record for the book is available from the British Library.
ISBN-13 978 0 470 51263 0
ISBN-10: 0 470 51263 6

REED PUBLISHING (NZ) LTD
TE KARUHI TĀ TĀPUI O REED (AOTEAROA)
Established in 1907, Reed is New Zealand's largest
book publisher, with over 600 titles in print.
www.reed.co.nz

Published under licence by Reed Books, a division of Reed Publishing (NZ) Ltd, 39 Rawene Road, Birkenhead, Auckland 0626. Associated companies, branches and representatives throughout the world.
A catalogue record for this book is available from the National Library of New Zealand.
ISBN-13 978 0 7900 978 1080 9
ISBN-10 0 7900 1080 1

© 2007 Penny Whiting
The author asserts her moral rights in the work.
First published 2007

Photos: Carlo Borlenghi, Francesco Ferri.
® The event logo of the 32nd America's Cup and the words 'America's Cup' are the property of America's Cup Properties Inc.

Designed by Ruby-Anne Fenning
Printed in China by Nordica

Contents

32nd America's Cup

Foreword

The modern-day America's Cup regatta has become more and more competitive, with performance margins between the top programmes decreasing all the time. The speed differences of previous Cups, which enabled a fast team to sail conservatively, are perhaps now in the past. Today we are looking for teams that have achieved the speed performance necessary to win and the ability to win on the race course come the day. This creates enormous pressure on the heads of the crews, the designers and the coaches over a long race programme. We look to see the next Cup being won by a crew that is better on the day.

The America's Cup bears some comparison with cricket and motor racing. The cricket comparison is the attempt to manage risk. Will a programme look to produce a boat optimised for 10 or 12 knots?, for upwind or downwind dominance?, for speed or for manouverability? What are the trade-offs of these benefits? The motor racing comparison is the requirement to use both intuitive design, analytical tools and technology to produce a fast boat that enables the crew (essentially the 'driver') to win the race. Penny Whiting's book will equip you with knowledge to interpret the 'game' and formulate your own opinions as a well-informed spectator.

Penny is an outgoing, ebullient, charming, outspoken, enthusiastic character, and loves the sea with a true passion. From a lifetime of being on the sea, in the sea, and passing her knowledge to thousands of others who wish to do the same, she has a developed a deep understanding of the ocean that is hard to surpass. Her parents are well-known in sailing circles, her brother is a successful yacht designer and her son is an America's Cup sailor and Star world champion. Penny's enthusiasm for the sea remains undiminished and her students, or perhaps I should call them friends, remain loyal and supportive.

Penny is uniquely equipped to open the door to America's Cup sailing to a wide audience. She knows many of the main players, and her ability to focus on what the 'game' is about, makes this book great reading.

Harold Cudmore
Isle of Wight
United Kingdom

What is the 32nd America's Cup?

The America's Cup Match is a match-racing series held approximately every three to four years between two teams, a **Defender** and a **Challenger**. The Defender is the winner of the previous America's Cup and the Challenger is the winner of a selection series, the Louis Vuitton Cup, which is held just before the America's Cup. The 32nd America's Cup format was designed to feature three distinct phases of racing; the so-called Louis Vuitton Acts, the Louis Vuitton Cup, and the 32nd America's Cup.

In 2000 the Defender was Team New Zealand because they had won the America's Cup in San Diego in 1995, against *Young America*. Team New Zealand was the Defender in 2003, when Alinghi won and took the cup to Switzerland. The Alinghi team then had the choice of where to sail the 2007 Challenge. Many European cities vied

> The Cup was made by Garrard & Sons in London in 1848.
> The 'Auld Mug' is a bottomless, silver ewer.
> It weighs in at 134 ounces (about 3.8 kilograms) and stands about 27 inches (68 centimetres) high.

to host the event, and the organisers eventually chose Valencia, Spain.

Teams race to be trustees of the silver trophy known as the America's Cup. In 1851 the yacht America won the inaugural trophy, giving life to the name for the challenge, the America's Cup. Since then the trophy has been contested at 31 events.

MATCH RACING AND FLEET RACING

Match races are races between two boats of the same class. In fleet racing it is possible to have large numbers of boats start and race together.

THE LOUIS VUITTON ACTS

The Acts are a series of races around Europe. The twelve teams race (including Alinghi), and the eleven challengers accrue points towards an overall Louis Vuitton Ranking. Challengers will earn bonus points based on their Ranking following Act 13. These points are added at the beginning of the Louis Vuitton Cup series. For the first time ever, the holder of the Cup, Alinghi, has been included in the racing, which will run until April 2007. After April, Alinghi will train alone. The first America's Cup race is programmed to start on 23 June 2007.

The challenger yachts match race as well as fleet race. Since 2003 they have sailed races in Marseille, France; Malmö-Skåne, Sweden; Trapani, Italy and Valencia.

THE LOUIS VUITTON CUP

Louis Vuitton, a Paris-based luggage and luxury-goods maker, became the sponsor of the Challenger Series in 1983. The first winner of the Louis Vuitton Cup was Australia II.

The Louis Vuitton Cup is awarded to the winner of the challenger series that is held before the America's Cup regatta. BMW Oracle was the first syndicate to challenge Alinghi for the 2007 America's Cup races. However, ten other teams also wish to challenge. A series of races over the last three sailing seasons has led to the Louis Vuitton Cup races in April 2007. The Louis Vuitton Cup will establish who will sail against the current holder of the America's Cup.

THE 32ND AMERICA'S CUP MATCH

Frequently referred to as The Match, this is the set of match races between the winning challenger and the current holder to determine who wins the America's Cup.

WHAT IS A TEAM?

A team is made up of anything between 60 and 150 people. The group includes designers, sailmakers, the weather team, shore crew, the sailing team and the group of people who handle the business and marketing side of running a team.

Today, there are huge corporations spending upward of US$90 million to race for the America's Cup. Historically, teams were funded by a few wealthy yacht club members, trials for the Cup would begin as little as four months before the actual Cup regatta, and the yachts would be sailed by amateur sailors.

Today's teams are fully paid employees. They stay together for the entire period of three or four years between Cup regattas. Being a member of a Cup team is a full-time job and career for those involved.

BOAT DESIGN

One of the most important aspects of team work is the boat design and new technology, which is an ongoing process. The introduction of the America's Cup-class yachts in 1995 showcased yachts that were suited for the conditions around the San Diego area — Pacific Ocean swells, which are quite large and often far apart and average winds of 5 to 12 knots but rarely more than 18 knots.

For the 2000 and 2003 America's Cup, the yachts had to be designed for New Zealand conditions — no ocean swells, flatter water, short chop and winds between 5 and 25 knots. **Hull**, **keel** and **rudder** designs were altered to suit New Zealand conditions, as were sail shapes.

Conditions in the Mediterranean require another style of yacht. The wind shifts a lot, with light sea breezes in the morning that regularly builld in the afternoons to 15 to 20 knots in strength. Quite often the sea state can change to a sharp, steep chop with a heavy swell, and winds can rise to 23 knots.

The design process is as important as any other aspect of an America's Cup campaign. A lot of time and effort goes into this process, along with a lot of secrecy! This is the reason the yachts wear 'skirts' that conceal the rudder and keel, essentially all of a yacht's underwater features.

In the past, the design process was the work of one designer or firm from outside the team who was responsible for hull, deck layout, keel and rudder design, a **mast** builder who would build the mast to fit the yacht, and a sailmaker who would design and build the sails. There was little communication between the three groups, therefore there was little co-ordination between these stages of construction and little idea of how it would all fit together.

Over the last 20 years, the design teams have become inclusive of all aspects of the yacht's construction. They work in close conjunction with each other at every step of the way. Computer-generated technical data gathered from the last America's Cup race is analysed and used when training their two boats. These two boats are usually an old boat and a 'new generation' vessel, which will test race over the years leading up to the next challenge. Collecting this data enables the team to quickly perfect the new yacht's performance.

BOAT MATERIALS

Materials for boat construction have changed from wood to aluminium to fibreglass to Kevlar, and now to carbon fibre. The same process has happened to sail materials: firstly constructed of cotton, then nylon and Dacron to Mylar with Kevlar and carbon fibre-moulded sails. Yacht materials have developed into a very high-tech industry that uses space-age and aviation materials and techniques. The boats are light and the keels are heavy. This combination helps make a fast boat.

WHY DO THE TEAMS HAVE TWO BOATS?

Using two boats from a previous campaign and all the information gathered about these boats, a well-funded team will build two new boats. These are of a new design using information gained from on-the-water sailing and tank and wind-tunnel testing.

In the past, the defending team had an advantage in that it usually did not have to compete in an elimination series, so it could reveal its yacht design later than the challengers. Today, the Acts span three seasons and are for all competitors. After Act 13 in April 2007, the Defender, Alinghi, will train alone. All Challengers sail in the Louis Vuitton Cup, and the winner of that series becomes the Challenger, who will sail against *Alinghi* in the 32nd America's Cup Match.

The teams for 2007

THE DEFENDER
SWITZERLAND
Yacht club Société Nautique de Genève
Team name Alinghi
Team head/s Ernesto Bertarelli
Sail number/s SUI 64, SUI 75, SUI 91, SUI 100
Yacht name *Alinghi*

THE CHALLENGERS
To date, there are eleven teams representing nine countries registered to challenge Alinghi for the 32nd America's Cup in 2007. The first yacht club to register was the Golden Gate Yacht Club in San Francisco (BMW ORACLE) and they negotiated the rules with the Société Nautique de Genève on behalf of the other challengers. The following information is as up-to-date as possible at the time of publication of this book.

USA

Yacht club   Golden Gate Yacht Club
Team name   BMW ORACLE Racing
Team head/s   Larry Ellison
Sail number/s   USA 71, USA 76, USA 87, USA 98

ITALY

Yacht club   Circolo Vela Gargnano
Team name   +39 Challenge
Team head/s   Lorenzo Rizzardi
Sail number/s   ITA 59, ITA 85

REPUBLIC OF SOUTH AFRICA (RSA)

Yacht club   Royal Cape Yacht Club
Team name   Team Shosholoza
Team head/s   Captain Salvatore Sarno
Sail number/s   RSA 83

NEW ZEALAND

Yacht club   Royal New Zealand Yacht Squadron
Team name   Emirates Team New Zealand
Team head/s   Grant Dalton
Sail number/s   NZL 81, NZL 82, NZL 84, NZL 92

ITALY

Yacht club   Yacht Club Italiano
Team name   Luna Rossa Challenge
Team head/s   Patrizio Bertelli
Sail number/s   ITA 74, ITA 80, ITA 86, ITA 94
Yacht name   *Luna Rossa*

FRANCE
Yacht club Cercle de la Voile de Paris
Team name Areva Challenge
Team head/s Stephane Kandler
Sail number/s FRA 57, FRA 60, FRA 93

SWEDEN
Yacht club Gamla Stans Yacht Sällskap — Stockholm
Team name Victory Challenge
Team head/s Hugo Stenbeck
Sail number/s SWE 63, SWE 73, SWE 96

SPAIN
Yacht club Real Federación Española de Vela
Team name Desafío Español 2007
Team head/s Agustin Zulueta
Sail number/s ESP 65, ESP 67, ESP 88, ESP 97
Yacht name Desafío Español

ITALY
Yacht club Reale Yacht Club Canottieri Savoia
Team name Mascalzone Latino — Capitalia Team
Team head/s Vincenzo Onorato
Sail number/s ITA 66, ITA 77, ITA 90, ITA 99

GERMANY
Yacht club Deutscher Challenger Yacht Club
Team name United Internet Team Germany
Team head/s Michael Scheeren
Sail number/s GER 72, GER 89

CHINA
Yacht club Qingdao International Yacht Club
Team name China Team
Team head/s Chaoyang Wang
Sail number/s CHN 69, CHN 79, CHN 95

Who makes the rules?

Deed of Gift

The Deed of Gift was presented to the New York Yacht Club with the silver cup in 1887 when the yacht *America* won the race. The Deed is the base rules documents for the America's Cup and has been modified throughout America's Cup history by Trustee Interpretive Resolution. It also allows for other rules and conditions to be agreed, by mutual consent, between the Defender and the Challenger. In recent events these rules have been incorporated in a document known as The Protocol. The Protocol is agreed before each America's Cup between the defending yacht club and the first yacht club to issue the challenge. The Deed states that the hull of the yachts taking part in the America's Cup must be constructed in the country of the challenging yacht club. All other equipment can be obtained from any source.

The Protocol
The Protocol becomes the governing document for the current America's Cup. It has been negotiated between the yacht club defending the Cup, Société Nautique de Genève, and the Challenger of Record, which is the first yacht club to register a challenge. For the 2007 America's Cup, the Challenger of Record is the Golden Gate Yacht Club, BMW ORACLE.
The Protocol outlines how the Louis Vuitton Cup and America's Cup regattas are to be run.
The Protocol has also established an America's Cup Jury to hear and rule on disputes between defenders and challengers. This was established to avoid disputes over the Deed of Gift going to the courts.

Finally, there are the racing rules. This are set out by the International Yacht Racing Federation for Match Racing. They specify how races are organised, run and raced.

International Match Racing Rules

The rules for racing are set out in the Notice of Race and Conditions issued by the present trustee of the Cup.

The International Sailing Federation issues the International Match Racing Rules. The America's Cup regatta may have modifications made to some rules, but these modifications have to be agreed to by both the Defender and the Challenger of Record for each regatta.

Umpires

Since 1992, on-the-water umpires have been used to see that the teams adhere to the rules. The umpires follow the yachts in chase boats. The aim of on-the-water-umpires is to avoid lengthy protests after the race.

In close-quarter situations, one of the yachts will always have **right of way**. The two umpires behind the respective yachts are constantly talking to each other to see if a yacht is in breach of the rules.

The umpire boats have lights, flags and a whistle to communicate with the racing yachts.

Penalties

Any violation of the rules is penalised on the water by the on-the-water umpires, as the race is being run. A penalty may require a yacht to perform a penalty turn (which is a circle from its present course). Whether the penalty is performed immediately or at another time during the race is indicated by coloured lights on the umpires' boat. A whistle and a flag are also used.

Protests

If there are any technical protests and disputes that are not dealt with by the on-the-water umpires and require a ruling after a race, each team is heard by a Jury that conducts a hearing. The Jury can assign penalties, including disqualification if a team is found to have violated the rules.

Strategy

A basic knowledge of the match-racing rules and terminology is helpful when watching the racing on television, because commentators use these rules to interpret what the boats are doing and why.

Yacht-racing strategy is a combination of an intimate knowledge of the rules, knowing how the boat works, the conditions and environment in which sailing is taking place, and an ability to anticipate where a rival is going to be and often trying to block that rival's moves!

The Races

THE LOUIS VUITTON CUP

Teams from around the world register their challenge and then race in the Louis Vuitton Acts, ahead of the Louis Vuitton Cup challenger selection series. The Louis Vuitton Acts were sailed in venues across Europe during the summers of 2004, 2005 and 2006, with the final, Act 13, to be sailed just ahead of the Louis Vuitton Cup in April 2007.

Ranking points are awarded throughout the Louis Vuitton Acts, with a weighting system making the later Acts more important. Based on the final ranking following Act 13, the eleven challengers are awarded bonus points to be carried into the Louis Vuitton cup.

The challengers can earn:

> 4 points for the leading challenger
> 3 points for the next three challengers
> 2 points for the next three challengers
> 1 point for the final four challengers

The Louis Vuitton Cup consists of two Rounds Robin, where each team sails each other challenger once. A win is worth two points. Based on Rankings at the end of the Round Robin Two, the top four challengers advance to a Semi-final, the winners of which sail in a Final for the Louis Vuitton Cup and the right to race Alinghi in the America's Cup. The Semi-finals, Final and the America's Cup Match are a series of up to nine races. The first team to prevail in five races is the winner.

A typical race day

After an early morning gym session, the crew arrives at the compound at around 8 a.m. The following schedule could differ on race days.

The crew get the two boats ready to launch (boats are always hauled out of the water after every sail to prevent marine growth adhering to the hull).

The **afterguard** (and sometimes the trimmers) consult with the weather team and plans are made on the expected forecast.

Each team meets and talks about the day.

Boats are launched and decisions are made about which sails go on the race yachts and what sails will go on the chase boat.

Both boats leave the base under tow, travelling down the new canal to the north or south race courses, which are easily seen outside the canal and boat bases.

Once near the course, both teams will put the sails on and start sailing together to check speeds and decide how they are going to handle the conditions of the day. At this point there is lot of communication with the weather team, who are strategically placed around the course. Choosing correct sail combinations on race day is very important.

As starting time nears, decisions must be made as to which sails need to be on the boat for the race and which sails will stay on the chase boat. The two boats sail **upwind** and **downwind** to check their speeds against each other. Seaweed and other debris can get caught on the keel **wings** or rudder; by sailing together they are able to check these things.

An America's Cup yacht usually has one **mainsail** aboard for each race, along with about seven **spinnakers**, including **asymmetricals**, and three or four **genoas**. They will often also carry a staysail. Final sail selection is often made immediately before preparation for the start line.

Communication with weather teams stops at the five minute gun.

Spectator boats have a defined area to watch from and they must keep well clear of the **starting box** and its surrounding area. This area is marked off with buoys and small boats.

Sometimes the race can be delayed or postponed due to the wind direction changing and/or too little or too much wind. The chase boats and the extra sails are never far away. Sometimes during a race a yacht will have to change to a different size of genoa if there is a significant change in wind strength on the upwind leg of the race. This is done by sliding one sail up a twin track on the forestay, while the other sail is still being used to sail the yacht. With fantastic crew work the other sail comes down and they are sailing with a different combination of sails because the conditions are different.

The Basics

It is helpful to know some basics of sailing when watching yacht racing.

1
....

A yacht cannot sail directly into the wind.

The nearest angle a normal yacht can sail to the wind is about 30° from the side the wind is coming from. However, the America's Cup yachts are so technically advanced that they can sail much closer to the wind.

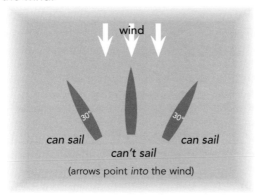

wind

30°   30°

can sail   can sail
can't sail

(arrows point *into* the wind)

If a yacht wants to get to where the wind is coming from it needs to tack from one side of the wind to the other. The tide, different strengths of wind at different angles and tactical positions with regard to the other boat govern when a boat will tack (or 'go about').

On a downward leg, direction is changed by **gybing**. Sailing upwind is also called on the wind, **beat**ing, **bash**ing, **slogging** or **close-hauled**.

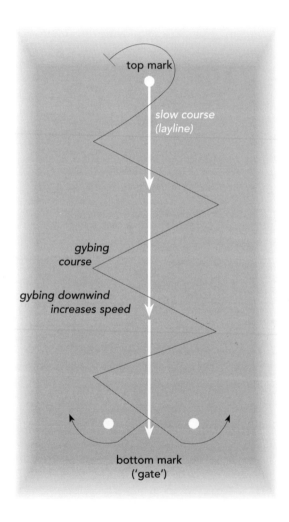

A yacht is on either port tack or starboard tack, depending on which side the wind hits the yacht. If the wind is coming from the port (left) side of the yacht, it is on the port tack. If the wind hits the starboard (right) side of the yacht, the boat is on the starboard tack. If the wind directly hits the back of the yacht and the main **boom** is to port (left), the yacht is on a starboard tack. If the wind directly hits the back of the yacht and the main boom is to starboard (right), the yacht is on port tack.

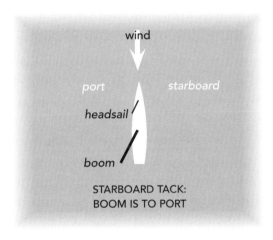

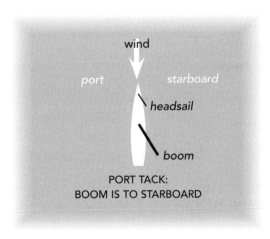

32nd America's CUP

America's Cup yacht sails are all measured and weighed by the race committee. A team will have up to 60 sails to choose from on race day. The sails are shaped like an aeroplane wing so that they give lift as well as forward movement. Both sails give these yachts power. The slot between the two sails is also very important to help the yacht sail closer to the wind and to the top mark of the course. Crew are constantly reshaping (or 'trimming') the sails to look like aeroplane wings as these provide the yacht's speed and power. Sailing downwind is when a yacht will put up the spinnaker (or asymmetrical sail), which flows out in front of the boat.

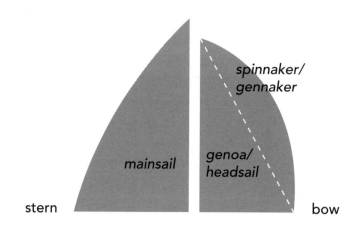

spinnaker/
gennaker

mainsail

genoa/
headsail

stern   bow

The further **forward** the angle the wind hits a yacht the further in the sails have to be. As the wind moves aft to the stern of the boat the sails go out until the wind is behind the boat. At this point the sails are all the way out.

When the wind hits a boat on the **beam** (the middle of the boat) the sails should be about halfway out.

In the America's Cup course, the yachts travel upwind or downwind. They often use wide angles going downwind for extra speed, rather than sailing straight to the bottom mark. This means they cover more distance than if they took a straight course, but because they are sailing faster, it is a more efficient strategy.

The less the rudder is turned, the better. Good sail **trim** stops the helmsman from having to turn the **wheel** (which is attached to the rudder) too much, as a turned rudder creates drag, acting a lot like a brake in a car if it is turned too much.

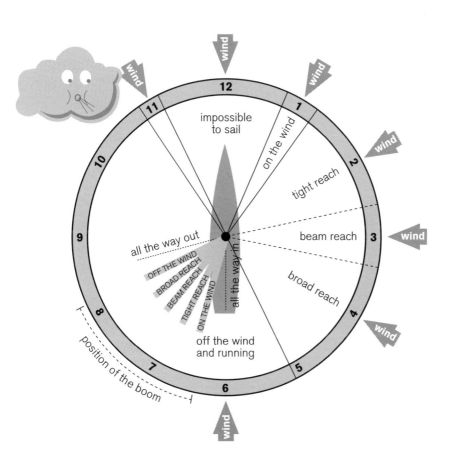

Points of sailing

The different angles to the wind on which a boat may sail (points of sailing)

off the wind	to sail downwind.
broad reach	with the wind aft, any point of sailing between a beam reach and running.
beam reach	wind hitting on the beam.
tight reach	wind just forward of the beam.
on the wind (close-hauled)	approximately 30° from the wind direction.
luffing	to bring the boat's head into the wind (the sail would luff, that is, flap like a flag).
running	to sail directly downwind with the sails eased right out.
boom	the spar attached to the bottom of the mainsail that pivots from the main mast.
leeward	to face away from the direction the wind is coming from.
windward	the direction from which the wind blows.

On page 25 a clock face is used to explain what point of sailing you are on. It's the same on both sides of the yacht; where the wind hits the yacht is that particular point of sailing.

The nearest angle you can sail to the wind is five-to or five-past the hour, and the sails are all the way in. The further aft the wind hits the boat, the further out the sails go.

Both sails are either all the way in or all the way out, or if the wind hits the boat on the beam, which is halfway, both sails are halfway out. All the way in is when you can't get the sails any further in.

Rules of Interest

There are some basic rules that determine which boat has the right of way. However closely the skipper and tacticians sail to the rules, they are always expected to leave the other yacht an avenue of escape and to take steps to avoid collision, even if they have right of way.

Right of way

There are two basic rules (these also apply to sailing in general, not just to match racing).

1   Port and starboard rule

Boats on **starboard** tack have right of way over boats on **port** tack. This means the wind is hitting them on the right side of the boat when they are on starboard tack, that is, both sails are on the left side.

2   Windward keeps clear of leeward

If both yachts are on the same tack with the wind on the same side, the **windward** boat is closer to where the wind is coming from and has to keep clear of the boat to **leeward** (where the wind is going). So, the leeward boat may push up the windward boat by **heading** them into the wind and forcing them to tack.

Overlap

An important aspect that applies in many situations determining right of way is **overlap**. This occurs when the following boat's **bow** (front) crosses the straight line from the lead boat's **stern** (back).

Crew members on the stern or bow of the boat indicate overlap by waving an outstretched arm up and down. In the diagram, the left-hand boat would normally give way to the boat on the right because they are to windward. However, because the following boat has overlapped the perpendicular line off the stern of the left-hand boat, the windward boat now has to keep clear.

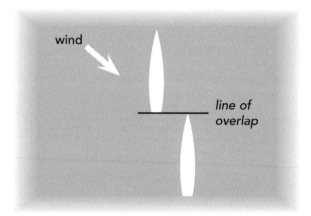

wind

line of overlap

Overlap is important when the yachts are going round the marks. If the yachts are on a downwind run, the following yacht might get an inside overlap (more than two boat lengths from the mark), which allows it to round first and be in a controlling position to start the upwind leg. The rules take into account which team created the overlap.

Some start line terminology

Backdown   When the crew quickly stops the yacht and gets it sailing slowly backwards to remove weed or plastic off the keel or rudder surfaces.

Dial-up   A manoeuvre by the starboard boat at the start to force the port boat to the least favoured end of the start area.

First cross   If the yachts have gone off on **split tacks** (different directions) at the start, the **first cross** is the first time the two yachts meet on opposite tacks. The yacht in first place crosses in front of the other yacht.

Layline   A layline is the best course the yacht is able to sail in order to get to the next mark without tacking or gybing.

Leverage   Teams constantly aim for more leverage or advantage against the opponent by using windshifts, knowing the most favoured end of the course, and employing sailing strategies.

Penalties The umpires give a penalty to the yacht infringing the rules. The penalty is usually a 270° turn. If the red penalty flag is flown the penalty turn must be completed as soon as possible. At other times the yachts can complete a penalty turn when they choose. If both yachts incur a penalty the penalties cancel each other out. Yachts have no rights on a penalty turn and will often try to come out on starboard tack.

Pin The start line is indicated with a committee boat at one end and a buoy at the other. The buoy is known as the pin.

Split tacks At the start line the yachts may go across the line on the same tack but then split off so one yacht is on starboard tack and one yacht is on port tack. This is a split tack.

Time on distance The time on distance is the time a yacht has to go until the start or from where they are to the next mark.

The start

The start sequence is possibly the most exciting part of the race and can have a huge impact on the rest of the race. Before the race there is a draw to decide which boat will approach the start line from the starboard end and which will approach from the port end of the line. The winner is able to decide their approach and this then alternates throughout the rest of the races between those two teams. This is known as alternating ends. The starboard approach boat flies a yellow flag from the **backstay** and the port-hand boat flies a blue flag.

Flags /Lights

The racing teams, race officials and umpires use several flags and lights on the umpire boats to signal to the racing boats. They use a whistle to alert the racing yachts to watch their flags and lights.

Blue LIGHT and Blue FLAG on umpire boat (plain blue flag)

Flown by the team approaching the start line from the port side. Used by the umpire when the blue team has incurred a penalty.

Yellow LIGHT and Yellow FLAG on umpire boat (plain yellow flag)

Flown by the team approaching the start line from the starboard end of the line. If it is held up by the umpire the yellow team has incurred a penalty.

1.   *Delayed penalties*   Unless a Red flag is displayed, a penalty may be undertaken at any time during the race.

2.   *Offset penalties*   If both yachts have a penalty they cancel each other out, unless a Red flag is displayed.

Red flag (plain red flag)

This is displayed with a blue or yellow flag and indicates that a team has to do a penalty turn immediately.

Green flag (green flag with white diagonal stripe)

Used by an umpire to indicate that no penalty is imposed.

Y flag (yellow and red diagonal stripes)

This is the protest flag displayed by a team to indicate to the umpires that they are protesting. The umpires then respond with the appropriate flag indicating their decision.

Black Flag (plain black flag)

Held up to show that a team is disqualified. The other team wins.

THE START SEQUENCE

The Race Committee Boat, which is at one end of the start line, uses flags and a horn and gun signal to time the start. The following start sequence is used:

1. Attention signal: 11 minutes to the start
   1 horn blow plus F flag
   (F flag is white with a red diamond at its centre)

2. Warning signal: 10 minutes to the start
   Horn plus Numerical Pennant flag for the number
   of the match due to start (replaces F flag)
   (Numerical Pennant One flag is white with red circle)

3. Preparatory signal: 5 minutes to the start
   Horn plus P flag. Both boats enter from respective ends.
   (P flag is blue with white square at centre)

4. One minute to start horn or gun
   P flag removed

5. Start signal
   1 horn and gun blow and Numerical Pennant flag removed.
   Numerical Pennant flag for the next match race is raised.
   (Numerical Pennant Two flag is blue with white circle)
   Port start boat = Blue flag
   Starbord start boat = Yellow flag
   Blue flag is raised if port boat is early, yellow flag is raised if starboard boat is yearly.

The rules require that the yachts have to enter the start area within two minutes of the preparatory signal and must enter from opposite sides of the start area. The boat that enters from the starboard side generally has the initial advantage because it enters the area with the right of way. It is able to control what the other boat does and may do the **dial-up** manoeuvre by heading straight for the port tack boat, forcing both boats to luff up into the wind. If it has the tactical and manoeuvring ability, it is able to continue controlling the other boat and force it to the least favoured end of the line.

The most favoured end of the line depends on the wind strength and direction and is decided on by the tactician and the skipper before entering the start area. This can mean that the first boat across the line may not necessarily have the best start. The other boat might be behind but upwind of the first boat and so be in the best position to use windshifts.

The 'winner' of the start is usually the boat that heads across the other on the first cross on the beat upwind. If the yachts go off on split tacks they may not cross until they are a long way up the first leg.

The port boat may engage in circling as a defence and force the starboard boat around the committee boat because the following boat is not able to go between it and the mark.

At the same time the skippers must be aware of their time on distance so that they always know how far they are away from the start, even if they are engaged in a duel with the other yacht to get to the favoured end of the line.

32nd America's CUP

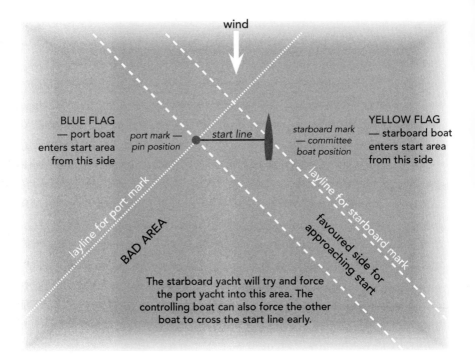

wind

BLUE FLAG
— port boat
enters start area
from this side

port mark —
pin position

start line

starboard mark
— committee
boat position

YELLOW FLAG
— starboard boat
enters start area
from this side

layline for port mark

BAD AREA

layline for starboard mark

favoured side for
approaching start

The starboard yacht will try and force
the port yacht into this area. The
controlling boat can also force the other
boat to cross the start line early.

THE UPWIND LEG

Understanding and predicting the strength and direction of the wind is the key to picking which is going to be the favoured side of the course and staying between the other competitor and the next mark, therefore forcing the competitor to the less-favoured side of the course. Match-racing strategy focuses on predicting wind changes (both direction of and strength) and on staying in the favoured position. However, predicting and picking windshifts is not easy and even at this level of racing involves a bit of luck.

The **upwind leg** means that the yachts have to tack (zigzag) up to the mark, which is set by the race committee to be directly upwind from the start.

The yacht that has the advantage will be looking to see how it can **cover** the other yacht to avoid it getting to the favoured side of the course and then get ahead of it. The trailing yacht may try to tack clear of the other yacht to create its own opportunities, but the leading boat will usually tack on top of it to control of the race. This is called **covering**. This kind of manoeuvring may continue right up to the top mark.

The tactician/strategist is constantly assessing the correct **layline** to approach the mark. The layline is the line the yacht can sail at maximum power straight to the mark without tacking. If the wind shifts, the layline shifts.

Approaching the top mark is a critical time. There are rules for going around marks. Firstly, the buoys must be approached so that the yachts go round them in a clockwise direction. Secondly, there is the 'two boat-length circle' rule. This is an imaginary line two boat-lengths from the mark. The normal starboard tack right of way rule does not apply within this circle if the boats are overlapped. Instead, as the outside boat must give room to the inside yacht whatever tack each is on.

THE DOWNWIND LEG

During the **downwind leg** the wind is behind the yacht. It can be a very important leg for the trailing yacht, which can block the wind of the boat ahead of it and may control the lead yacht's course and position.

Going downwind, the boats almost never sail directly towards the next mark because they can go faster by **gybing** downwind. The lighter the wind, the greater the angle at which the boat has to sail to maximise its speed. Although the yachts may seem to be able to sail straight to the mark, the fastest time to the mark is not necessarily via a straight line.

Choosing the correct sails and course is critical. If the wind is strong a spinnaker may be set, or in lighter winds the asymmetrical sail is used. Both sails are huge and gybing requires skilled sail-handling from the crew.

After going around the mark the yacht will either do a **bear away set** (meaning the crew sets the spinnaker or asymmetrical as they go around the mark) or do a **gybe set** (meaning they set the spinnaker after they have **gybe**d). The latter is slower because the boat loses speed as it gybes.

Approaching the bottom mark the yachts again have to adhere to the three-boat-length rule. Being between the other yacht and the mark is the favoured position because the rules state that a yacht must be allowed room around the mark. The outside boat has to give way and may be forced to sail a wider, longer course around the mark.

The last leg of the race is always a downwind run.

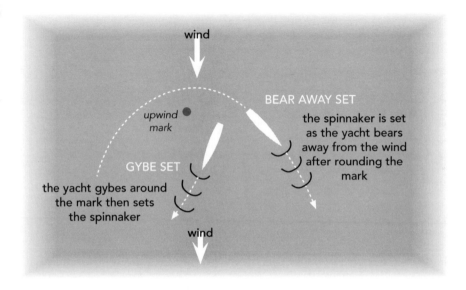

The Yachts

All yachts that have raced in the Louis Vuitton and America's Cup since 1988 are in a specific class known as the International America's Cup Class (IACC). These boats must conform to the IACC rules. These rules have evolved due to controversy surrounding the interpretation of previous rules and because of races being held between extremely different boats. The first IACC yachts (now called ACC yachts) raced in the America's Cup in 1992 in San Diego.

> The design parameters of the rules mean that while each boat is not identical, they are capable of similar performance. The aim is to have different boats racing on equal terms.

Formula

There is an extremely strict formula that allows different yachts to race competitively. The formula sets out certain measurements for length, sail area and **displacement.** Each of these dimensions has the ability to make a boat go faster, but the rule is designed so that an increase in one dimension tends to cause a penalty in another. All yachts are inspected by the Technical Director during construction and before and during racing. A team outside the formula can be disqualified.

Most America's Cup yachts are just short of 25 metres in length, with a beam of around 4 metres. The mast is about 32 metres, above deck. The boats carry about 350 square metres of sail upwind, and about 700 square metres downwind. The entire boat weighs about 24 tons and about 80 percent of the yacht's weight is in the bulb. The lighter the team makes the hull, the more weight can be in the bulb, increasing stability and speed.

The hull

The current boats are **monohulls** (one hull). They are constructed out of layers of carbon fibres and 'baked' to be very strong but light.

They have a number of appendages — **fins, rudders, bulbs** and **wings.** Fittings below the water contribute to drag so they have to be considered carefully. The design of the **keel** has become very important and there is a special day nominated, 1 April 2007, on which each syndicate must reveal its keel.

The sails

The sails usually carried on board for a race day are one mainsail, three or four genoas, seven asymmetrical sails and spinnakers, and often a staysail. However, these numbers will vary according to wind speed on the day. There is a weight limit of 650 kilograms of sail allowable on a boat and crew will decide what sails they want to carry each day, bearing in mind that weight limit.

Each yacht receives a consecutive class number that is displayed on its sail with the silhouette of the America's Cup above (this silhouette is the class insignia).

Boat terminology

1. aft — at or near the stern.
2. beam — the widest part of the boat.
3. forward — forward section of the boat.
4. bow — the front end of the boat.
5. port — the left side of the boat when looking forward.
6. starboard — the right side of the boat when looking forward.
7. stern — the rear end of the boat.

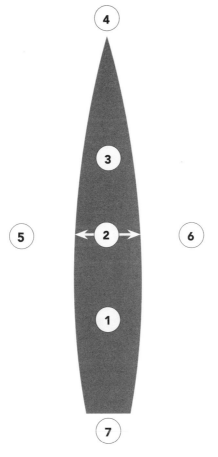

Parts of the boat — rigging

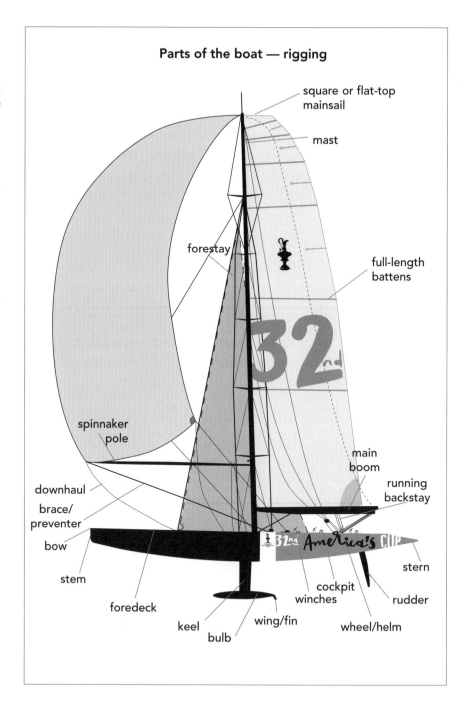

square or flat-top
mainsail

mast

forestay

full-length
battens

spinnaker
pole

main
boom

running
backstay

downhaul

brace/
preventer

bow

stern

stem

cockpit
winches

rudder

foredeck

keel

wing/fin

wheel/helm

bulb

Sails and sheets

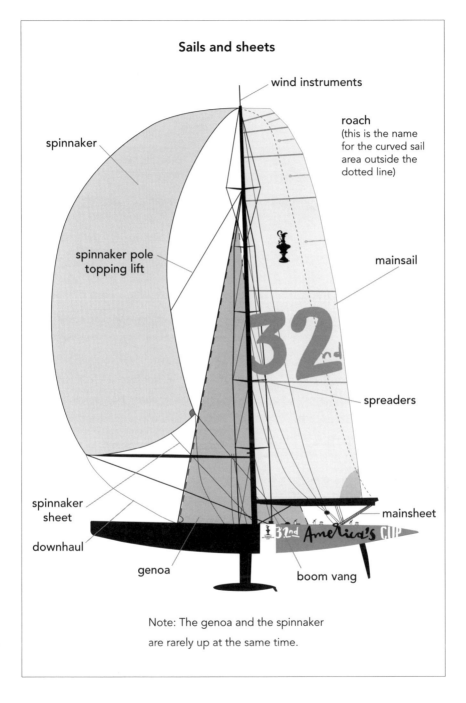

wind instruments

roach
(this is the name for the curved sail area outside the dotted line)

spinnaker

spinnaker pole topping lift

mainsail

spreaders

spinnaker sheet

downhaul

genoa

boom vang

mainsheet

Note: The genoa and the spinnaker are rarely up at the same time.

Boat measurements

The America's Cup Class (ACC) has been updated through Version 5 of the Class Rule, with the changes making the boats lighter, more nimble, and quicker to accelerate.

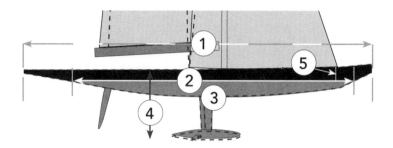

1. **Length Overall (LOA)**   a boat's extreme length, measured from the foremost part of the bow to the aftermost part of the stern, approximately 25 metres.

2. **Beam**   approximately 4 metres.

3. **Waterline Length (LWL)**   the length of a boat at the waterline from stern to stern; **Wetted Surface**   the area of the hull under water. Hull weight is approximately 5 tons.

4. **Draft**   (approx. 4.1 m) the depth of water a boat requires in order to float. This is the vertical distance from the waterline to the bottom of the keel. Keel weight is approximately 19 tons.

5. **Topsides/Freeboard**   the height of the side of the boat from the waterline to the deck.

Year 2003 (Version 4 ACC)

Year 2005–2007 (Version 5 ACC)

Mast height is approximately 33 metres above the deck. Overall weight is approximately 24 tons.

The Crew

**Each yacht is required to
have 17 crew members.**

A crew trains for years in preparation for the final regatta. Although each person has a clear role, the emphasis is on teamwork, fitness and endurance. Each crew member is required to be a good sailor who is strong, very fit and committed.

There can be one other person aboard who must not participate in any aspect of the race or sailing. This person usually sits behind the afterguard, at the back end of the yacht, and is referred to as the 18th man or the owner's representative, guest or sponsor.

1. *Bowman*

The bowman is involved in a number of roles. In a prestart manoeuvre he will be up on the bow calling time and distance to the starting line and conveying other important information about the start line and the opponent back to the afterguard. Some of his communications will be handsignals. He also attaches **halyards** to hoist sails and sheets to control the sails. Often in prestart he will help control the genoa by backing it against the wind to stall the yacht. He organises the **foredeck** for the next sail hoist.

2 and 3. *Midbow/sewer*

On deck, the midbows work with the mast and pit crew during sail changes. The midbows run the 'sewer' (see position 3) below decks. They are responsible for the packing and stowing of all sails before and after changes.

4. *Pitman*

The pitman calls the halyard tension. When the sail is completely hoisted, he works in conjunction with the foredeck crew. He also pulls the halyards that are being pulled by the mastman, controls ropes in the cockpit for the bowman and is the communication link to the crew that run the front of the yacht. He eases halyards for the dropping of the sails.

5. *Mastman*

The mastman is the big guy who helps the bowman and the midbowman. He leaps in the air and grabs the halyard (this action is called 'bouncing') to pull up the new sail at mark roundings or sail changes with the halyard at the mast, before the halyard goes to the grinders to be fully hoisted. He is also responsible for attaching the spinnaker pole to the mast as well as helping to gybe and to store the spinnaker pole. He is also involved in trimming and grinding the mainsail.

6 and 7. *Grinders (two people)*

This group is also called the 'engine room'. The grinders respond to instructions to winch in the sail. They bring the sail in by grinding in on huge manual winches called coffee grinders (the yachts are not allowed electric winches). Grinders also hoist the mainsail and genoas using the coffee grinders. There can be up to eight people grinding at one time. Without grinders the yacht is powerless.

8 and 9. *Trimmers*
The correct trim of sails is one of the most vital aspects of a fast boat. A trimmer needs to be fit and strong and will have years of match-racing experience. There are two trimming positions for travelling upwind and downwind. Trimming the sails has everything to do with ensuring the correct sail shape, as good sail shape provides maximum power and boat speed. Experienced sailmakers sometimes make the best trimmers as they understand the shapes of the sails.

The trimmers of the **headsails** (the genoas and the spinnakers) work closely with the mainsail trimmer and the helmsman. Headsail trim is important for the balance and manoeuvrability of the yacht. Their trimming functions change according to whether the yacht sails upwind or downwind.

A spinnaker is used only on the downwind legs of the course. It is a large billowing sail that requires careful trimming. The aim is to keep the large sail full so the trimmer is constantly letting the sail out and bringing it in. The trimmer calls the sail and the grinders work the **winches** to control the sheets that bring the sails in again.

10. *Mainsail grinder*
Works in with the trimmer and the helmsman. This position requires someone very strong as their power is critical for steering and control of the boat.

11. *Mainsail trimmer*
Because the mainsail is so big — measuring between 200 and 225 square metres — it contributes significantly to the yacht's performance.

The mainsail trimmer works closely with the helmsman, the headsail trimmers and the strategist to ensure the correct trim of the mainsail is allowing the yacht maximum speed.

12. *Runnerman*

The wires that tighten the backstays are called the runners. They run from the stern of the boat up the mast. The tension of the backstays is crucial to the performance of the boat and for making sure the mast stays upright.

The runner is let go when the yacht tacks from one side of the wind to the other. The windward runner has to be winched tight during this manoeuvre.

13. *Traveller man*

The mainsheet traveller is a metal track running across the yacht in front of the steering position. The track transfers the load of the sail from the sail to the helm of the yacht and is important for control of the yacht.

The traveller and mainsail trimmer work closely together to determine the correct mainsail shape and position.

14. *Helmsman (or skipper)*

The skipper is responsible for the boat and making the ultimate decisions after receiving information and advice on how the boat is sailing from the navigator, the tactician and the sail trimmers. The helmsman steers the boat. Often the skipper and the helmsman are the same person. The afterguard (the navigator and tactician) and the helmsman call **tactics** in the prestart positioning and in situations where they and the other boat are in close quarters.

15. *Navigator*

The navigator uses information from computers and instruments to make sure that the boat is on course, sailing the best course and speed for the start, rounding the marks and crossing the finish line. The navigator communicates with the helmsman, the tactician and the sail trimmers about time on distance, times to marks, laylines and general information regarding wind patterns.

16 and 17. *Tactician and strategist*

The strategist and tactician are key members of the crew. The tactician concentrates on the tactical position of the boat in relation to the position of its competition, and plans where his own boat wants to be on the race track. He relays this important information to the helmsman and the navigator.

The strategist knows the overall plan; he communicates with the on-the-water weather team before the race and also assists the tactician. The strategist is always looking up the course for any changes in conditions.

The tactician and the strategist have an intimate knowledge of race rules and they carefully consider sea, wind and tide change conditions.

The Course

In 2007, the Louis Vuitton Cup and the 32nd America's Cup Match will be raced at Valencia, Spain, which is in the Mediterranean. The yachts will race in winds between 7 and 23 knots.

The races in the Louis Vuitton Cup are held on the North or South courses.

For the 32nd America's Cup Match, it is intended for the North Race Area to be used.

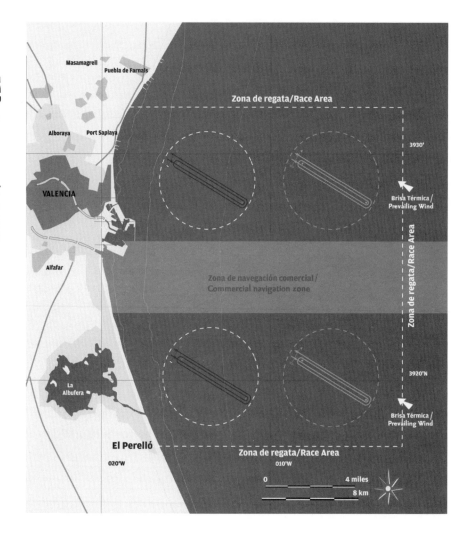

The actual position of the race course will depend on weather conditions, as illustrated in this diagram that includes the Spanish terms.

RACE LENGTH

The length of a race can vary depending on conditions. The course will be between 8.6 and 12.6 nautical miles, taking around 1 hour and 30 minutes.

There are four legs in each race, as shown in the diagram opposite.

The first and last legs, when the yachts cross the start/finish line, are approximately 3 nautical miles long.

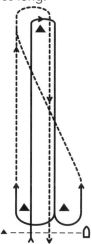

Fleet racing

Several of the Louis Vuitton Acts are fleet races, an innovation in America's Cup racing. The diagram following shows the course a fleet race follows.

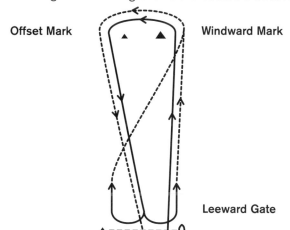

Offset Mark   **Windward Mark**

Leeward Gate

SPECTATORS

There are restrictions on where spectators in boats may be in relation to the races, as well as speed restrictions.

Spectator boat restrictions

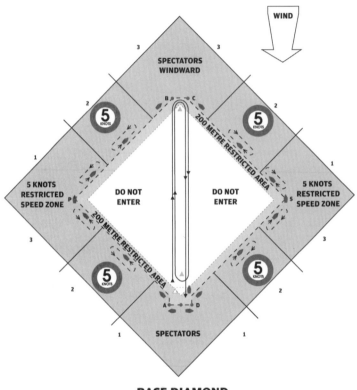

RACE DIAMOND

A short history of the America's Cup

The first challenge

During the late 1840s, American John Cox Stephens and five friends built a **schooner** named *America* that was very different from traditional yacht design at the time. They issued a race challenge to the Royal Yacht Squadron in England.

The Royal Yacht Squadron ran the race around the Isle of Wight, which was its island base. The prize for the winner was a silver trophy named the 100 Guineas Cup.

On 22 August 1851, the American yacht America won the race with a large lead. In 1857 a member of the 1851 winning syndicate gave the 'America's Cup' (so-named after *America* won it) to the New York Yacht Club with the original Deed of Gift, thus establishing the idea of an international regatta between yacht clubs.

America versus England

Since the first challenge in 1870, the Cup has been a fiercely contested trophy. There have been regular challengers, about every three or four years, with large gaps around the time of the two world wars. The New York Yacht Club remained the Defender of the cup for 113 years.

Until the 1980s, competition was primarily between England and America, but England has never been successful.

One explanation has been the different approach each nation took towards the race. England's approach involved a belief in sport as the pursuit of amateurs with **Corinthian** yachting ethics and sportsmanship. This contrasted with the hard-nosed, professional ethics the Americans employed in all aspects of the defence, utilising the best designers and sailors in an all-out pursuit of victory.

Bigger and bigger

From the first challenge in 1870, until the Second World War, the yachts became progressively bigger. In order to be as fast as possible, the boats had a long **waterline length (wl),** one mast, and they were gaff-rigged (meaning they had a four-sided mainsail) with a **topsail** above that. The ultimate long boat with huge rigs was *Reliance*, the Defender in 1903.

Designed by Nathanael Herreshoff, *Reliance* had a length overall of nearly 144 feet (40 metres). Her mast towered at 196 feet (60 metres) with over 16,000 square feet (1500 square metres) of sail. Herreshoff's innovative approach included two steering wheels, a hollow rudder that could be filled with water or pumped hollow for easier steering, winches with gears and ball bearings, lightweight steel **spar**s and a **topmast** that could be lowered into the **mainmast** if it wasn't being used.

Reliance raced against the Challenger *Shamrock III*. This was Sir Thomas Lipton's third America's Cup challenge. Lipton challenged for the Cup five times but had no success.

In 1930, the year the J-boat era began. J-boats were built to the J-class rule, which specified a waterline length between 75 and 87 feet and a single mast. The rig underwent a dramatic change from gaff (four-sided) to three-sided Bermudan sails. The Bermudan is still the standard sail on America's Cup boats as they perform well into the wind, are efficient and require less rigging. The American Defender, *Enterprise*, won the regatta, which was Sir Thomas Lipton's last.

The 1930s saw some close, exciting racing. The yachts were huge and demanded competent skippers and crew. In 1934 England came the closest they ever had to winning the Cup. They went into the 1937 challenge determined to win.

Aware of the English effort to succeed, Harold Vanderbilt built *Ranger*. With a steel hull, *Ranger* was very powerful and very fast, and she is the most famous J-boat. She had the maximum allowable waterline length of 87 feet, and a 165-foot mast made of duralumin. *Ranger* made a clean sweep of the series against the Challenger, *Endeavour II*. Sadly, *Ranger* was broken up during the Second World War for steel and lead. Of the America's Cup J-boats, only *Shamrock III* and *Endeavour II* survive.

Smaller but better

The next America's Cup was in 1958. Taking into consideration the economic climate and the huge cost of the J-boats, the Royal Yacht Squadron was asked by the Americans to recommend a smaller, less expensive racing yacht. These boats were called by the misnomer '12-metres', even though they were the largest racing yachts of the time. The name 12-metre referred to the International Rule requiring that the dimensions of the boat's length, beam, sail area and **topsides/freeboard** added up to 12 metres. Compared to the J-boats they were tiny, as they had a 45-foot waterline length and 1900 square feet of sail. They were actually about 20 metres in length.

The 12-metre era (1958–87) carried on the tradition of important advances in boat building and design. Some of these advances are now common aspects of modern yachts, including the reverse **transom**, and bulb keels.

The first regattas of this era were raced without much fuss as the Americans kept its grip on the trophy. This began to change with the arrival of teams from Australia.

New challengers

In 1970, for the first time, multiple challenges were received and trials were held between France and Australia. It was a contentious regatta. There were several wrangles between the challengers and the defenders and a nasty collision in the final race between Challenger *Gretel II* and Defender *Intrepid*. The incident stirred Australian resolve to bring the Cup to the Southern Hemisphere.

After participating in four more regattas, Australia's victory in the 1983 regatta ended the New York Yacht Club's control over the America's Cup. *Australia II* will be most remembered for her winged keel and the subsequent controversy about how legal and within the 12-metre rule it was. Dennis Conner, the skipper of the Defender *Liberty*, was the first American skipper to lose the America's Cup in 132 years.

The Royal Perth Yacht Club was the first successful Challenger of the America's Cup and held the next regatta off their homeport of Fremantle in Western Australia in 1987. Conner's determination to reclaim the Cup paid off and he won the regatta.

The race in 1988, held off the west coat of America by the San Diego Yacht Club, was the most controversial in a long history of controversial racing. Two years of acrimonious court battles between New Zealander Michael Fay's Big Boat challenge and Dennis Conner resulted in a mismatch between a large, heavy **sloop** and an ultra-light **catamaran**. It also resulted in officials agreeing to a new set of rules for future regattas that would prevent similar, costly disputes.

Lighter and faster

The modern era of the America's Cup had arrived. The new International America's Cup Class yachts were lighter and faster than the 12-metre boats. In the first America's Cup using IACC boats in 1992, some teams built up to five boats. Later, teams were limited to two new boats within a Cup cycle to conduct their campaigns. An international jury was set up. On-the-water umpires keep the competition tight, out of jury rooms and away from protest panels. Women, virtually invisible for over 100 years, were included in sailing crews.

In 1995, Team New Zealand challenged and won the Cup in *NZL 32*. After a 37-1 record in the Louis Vuitton Cup, Team New Zealand won 5-0 in the America's Cup regatta, leading the final race by six minutes.

In 2000, Team New Zealand again won the America's Cup with a 5-0 record, beating the Italian yacht *Luna Rossa* in the Defender's Series. New Zealand is now the only country other than America to successfully defend the Cup.

Alinghi, winner of the 2003 America's Cup challenge, was specifically designed to win in New Zealand, carrying huge tolerances against the large variety of sailing conditions in New Zealand waters.

Although it has changed from a one-race event with one challenger and several defenders, to a match-racing regatta between one defender and competing challengers, the America's Cup has lost none of its mystique or challenge. It continues to provide a focus for yachting design and technology and is one of the ultimate challenges for sailors around the world.

Port America's Cup
Interior, Valencia

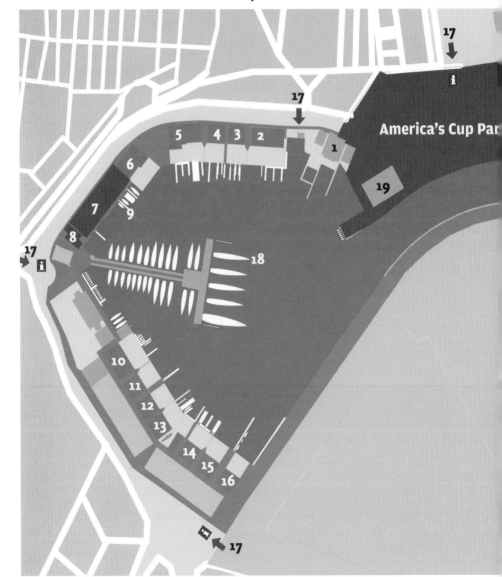

1	Organisation offices
2	Alinghi
3	+39 Challenge
4	Team Shosholoza
5	BMW ORACLE Racing
6	Luna Rossa Challenge
7	There is no Second: from *America* to *Alinghi*
8	House of the America's Cup
9	Public spectator boats
10	Emirates Team New Zealand
11	Areva Challenge
12	Victory Challenge
13	Desafío Español 2007
14	United Internet Team Germany
15	Mascalzone Latino — Capitalia Team
16	China Team
17	Entrance
18	Superyacht marina
19	Veles e Vents building

A beginner's guide to sailing terminology

aback	describes a sail that the wind has struck on its back or wrong side. This would be caused by a wind change or a course change.
abeam	at right angles to the middle of a boat.
Acts	series of races teams compete in prior to the Louis Vuitton Cup. Properly called Louis Vuitton Acts.
aft	at or near the stern.
afterguard	(also called the 'brainstrust') the group comprising the helmsman, strategist, navigator, tactician, and the man up the mast.
apparent wind	a combination of true wind speed and the boat speed when sailing upwind.
astern	behind the boat; to go astern is to steer the boat in reverse or backwards.
back a sail	to force a sail against the wind (sometimes by physically leaning against the boom). This manoeuvre is used to make a boat stop or slow down.

backdown	turning very quickly to stop a yacht and slowly reversing to clear weed or plastic from the keel or rudder.
backing	when the wind moves counter-clockwise.
backstay	wire from the top of the mast to the stern of the boat to hold the mast up.
ballast	heavy weight, usually iron or lead, which is placed low in the boat to provide stability.
bash	see beat/bash
batten	flexible strip of fibreglass inserted horizontally into a batten pocket in the outside edge of the sail to give the sail shape and support.
beam	the widest part of a boat.
bear away	to steer away from the wind.
bear away set	to set the spinnaker without gybing when rounding the mark.
beat/bash	to sail on a zigzag course, tacking upwind.
bilge	the lower inside area of the hull.
boom	the spar to which the foot of a mainsail is attached.
boom vang	a system used to hold the boom down, particularly when a yacht is sailing downwind, so that the surface of the mainsail facing the wind is at a maximum.
bow	the front of the boat.
brace/preventer	line and tackle that limits the movement of the boom, usually for reasons of safety (so the boom doesn't knock a sailor overboard).
broach	to heel over so the rudder comes out of the water, limiting steerage.
broad reach	with the wind aft, any point of sailing between a beam reach and running.
bulb	the lump of lead at the bottom of the keel to stabilise the yacht.

catamaran	a sailing boat with two hulls.
Challenger	a team challenging the current Defender of the America's Cup.
circling	a tactic where two boats circle at the same time, chasing each other to gain the advantage.
clear air	wind that is not disturbed by an opponent.
clew	the after, lower corner of a sail at the junction of the foot and leech.
close quarters	sailing very close together.
close-hauled	the point of sailing closest to the wind (30°). The sails are all the way in.
cockpit	the area behind the mast where the crew work.
Corinthian	a nineteenth and early twentieth century term for an amateur yachtsman.
course	the direction in which a vessel is steered or is steering.
cover	where a leading boat is directly to windward of the other boat and it disturbs the airflow onto its opponent. The trailing boat is forced to tack in the opposite direction to escape the disturbed wind going up- or downwind.
Cunningham	crinkle just above the tack to flatten the sail. It changes the shape of the sail, moving the airflow forward.
current	flow of water caused by tide or wind movement of the sea.
dead run	running with the wind blowing behind it.
deck	the covering over the hull used to walk on.
Deed of Gift	the original set of rules (1871) for the America's Cup.
Defender	the team defending its possession of the America's Cup.
dial up	a manoeuvre by the starboard boat at the start to force the port boat to the least favoured end of the start area.
dipping/dip/duck	a sudden change of course to pass behind another boat.

displacement	the weight of seawater displaced by the submerged part of the boat and which is exactly equal to the boat's weight.
downhaul	a rope fitted to pull down the spinnaker boom.
downwind	sailing a course with the wind behind.
downwind leg	sailing away from the wind; to round a bottom mark.
downwind mark	the mark at the bottom of the course.
draft	the depth of water a boat requires in order to float, being the vertical distance from the waterline to the bottom of the keel.
dummy tacks	*see false tacks*
eye of the wind	the direction from which the wind is coming. Also called the true wind.
false tacks	also called dummy tacks. A tactic to trick the other boat whereby a trailing boat performs only half a tack and then returns to its original course without going about. To stop a cover.
fins	*see wings/fins*
first cross	if the boats have gone off on split tacks (different directions) at the start, the first cross is the first time that the two boats go past each other.
foot	the bottom edge of the sail between the tack and clew.
foredeck	the deck area forward of the mast.
forestay	the foremost stay, running from the masthead to the bow.
foretriangle	also called the J measurement. The triangle formed between the mast, forestay and the deck.
forward	forward section of boat.
freeboard	height of the side of the boat from the waterline to the deck.

gennaker	an asymmetric spinnaker used in lighter breezes when sailing downwind.
genoa	a large headsail, which overlaps the mast.
go about	to turn the boat through the eye of the wind to change tack.
gybe	to change tack by turning away from the wind; by turning the bow of the boat towards the main boom, the mainsail goes to the opposite side.
gybe set	to go around a mark, gybe, and then set a spinnaker or gennaker.
halyard	rope or wire used to hoist and lower sails.
head	top of the sail attached to the halyard.
head to wind	the bow of the boat headed directly into the true wind.
heading	the direction the boat is heading according to the compass.
headsails	the genoas and the jibs.
heel	the leaning over of the boat due to pressure of the wind on the sails.
helm	another word for the tiller or wheel of a boat that steers it.
hull	the main body of a boat.
hull speed	theoretical maximum speed of a boat relative to its overall length.
in irons	describes a boat stalled head-to-wind.
J measurement	*see* foretriangle
keel	underwater appendage that gives the yacht stability and lift going to windward.

layline	the best course the yacht is able to sail in order to get the next mark without tacking or gybing.
lee/leeward	away from the wind.
leech	the after edge of the sail from head to clew.
leeway	the sideways drift of a boat (that is, sailing to windward).
length overall (loa)	the boat's extreme length, measured from the foremost part of the bow to the aftermost part of the stern.
leverage	teams constantly aim for more leverage or advantage against the opponent by using windshifts, knowing the most favoured end of the course, and by employing sailing strategies.
luff	the forward edge of a sail.
luff up	bring the boat into the wind.
luffing	when a sail flaps like a flag.
mainmast	the single vertical spar that the sails and a boom are attached to.
mainsail	the sail attached to the mast and the boom.
mainsheet	a rope that controls mainsail shape. It is attached to the main boom. This sheet pulls the mainsail in and lets it out.
mainsheet traveller	a fitting that slides sideways in a track and is used to alter the angle of the mainsail.
mark	a buoy in the water.
mast	a vertical spar that holds up a sail or sails.
mast step	the place at which the bottom of the mast is fitted in the hull.
midships	area around the middle of the boat.
monohull	boat with only one hull.
off the wind	sailing downwind.
on the wind	sailing upwind.
overlap	when the following boat's bow crosses the lead boat's stern.

penalty	the umpires give a penalty to a boat infringing the rules.
pin	the start line is indicated with a committee boat at one end and a buoy at the other. The buoy is known as the pin.
port	the left side of the boat when looking forward.
pressure	wind strength.
rail	edge of the deck where the crew sit and where the deck meets the hull.
reach	to sail with the wind roughly on the beam.
rig	sails, mast and stays.
right of way	the boat which is on the starboard tack or which is windward yacht has the right of way.
roach	the curved portion of a sail extending past a straight line drawn between two corners.
round robin	a series of races where a team races every other team once.
rudder	a flat appendage at the rear of the boat, in the water, to steer the boat.
running	to sail directly downwind with the sails eased out.
running rigging	all of the moving lines such as halyards and sheets used in the support and control of sails and booms.
sail set	every time a boat changes its course it will change its sail set or shape.
schooner	a boat with two masts, the shortest mast forward.
sea room	the room in which a boat can manoeuvre without danger of collision or going aground.
sheet	a rope controlling the shape of a sail.
sidestay/shroud	wires, usually in pairs, reaching from the mast to the sides of the boat to prevent the mast falling sideways.
slogging	tacking upwind.

sloop	a single-masted boat with a mainsail and one headsail.
spar	a general term for mast, booms and poles.
spinnaker	a large, light, balloon-shaped sail set in front of the bow when the boat is off the wind.
split tack	at the start line the boats may go across the line on the same tack but then split off so one boat is on starboard tack and one boat is on port tack. This is a split tack. It can also occur during a race.
spreaders	horizontal struts attached to the mast, which spread the shrouds out from the mast and improve their support of the mast.
starboard	the right side of the boat when looking forward.
start box	the area around the start boat and start line, well-marked by buoys.
stem	the bow of the boat between the deck and the waterline.
stern	the rear end of the boat.
tack (sail)	the lower forward corner of the sail.
tack (movement)	to change the boat from one side of the wind to the other, by either gybing or going about.
tactics	using boating rules, the sea and the wind to one's advantage.
telltails	pieces of thread attached to strategic parts of the sails to indicate air flow and sail lift.
tender	smaller boat used to take crew, sails and gear on and off the boat.
tight covering	where the lead boat matches the trailing boat tack for tack.
tight reach	the wind is just forward of the beam.
time on distance	the time a boat has to go until the start or from where it is to the next mark.
topmast	the very top of a spar that can be bent to flatten the mainsail.

topping lift	rope or wire used to adjust boom height.
topsides/ freeboard	the sides of a boat between the waterline and the deck.
track	the course a boat has made on the water.
track slides	these attach the mainsail to the mast.
transit lines	transit lines are used by tacticians and skippers to assess the best layline for the start, to a mark or to another boat.
transom	the flat surface forming the stern of the boat.
trim	to adjust the angle of the sails by means of sheets, so that they are at their best shape and angle to the wind.
true wind	where the wind comes from when boat is not moving.
true wind speed	the wind speed from a stationary point on the water (as opposed to apparent wind speed).
upwind	towards the wind.
upwind leg	the leg of a course that heads to where the wind is coming from.
veer	when the wind direction shifts clockwise.
velocity made good (vmg)	the speed a boat is making relative to the position of a mark. When sailing upwind the best vmg is between 30° and 20° and when sailing downwind the best vmg is between 135° and 170°.
wake	the disturbed water left behind a boat.
waterline length (LWL)	the length of a boat from stem to stern at the waterline.
weather side	the side of a boat on which the wind is blowing.
wetted surface	the area of the hull and other appendages under water.
wheel	see helm

winches	large drums that are used to winch in and hoist sails.
windward	the direction from which the wind blows.
windward mark	the mark of the course set upwind from the start line.
wings/fins	attachments at the bottom of a keel used for stability, to create lift and to help steering.

32nd America's CUP

VALENCIA
32nd AMERICA'S CUP

LOUIS VUITTON
E endesa
Santander
Alcatel·Lucent

SUPPORTERS
Nespresso
Adecco
Ford
El Corte Inglés
Estrella Damm
Grupo Leche Pascual
Coca-Cola
Vodafone

2007 Programa de

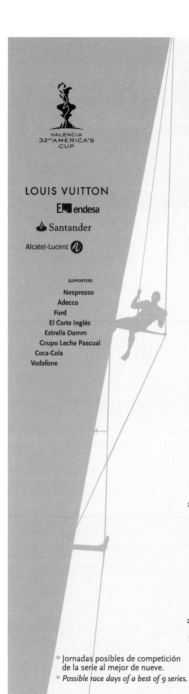

Abril | *April*

1 Dom|*Sun*	
2 Lun|*Mon*	
3 Mar|*Tue*	
4 Mie|*Wed*	Valencia Louis Vuitton Act 13
5 Jue|*Thu*	
6 Vie|*Fri*	
7 Sáb|*Sat*	Día de reserva *Reserve Day*
8 Dom|*Sun*	
9 Lun|*Mon*	
10 Mar|*Tue*	
11 Mie|*Wed*	
12 Jue|*Thu*	
13 Vie|*Fri*	
14 Sáb|*Sat*	
15 Dom|*Sun*	
16 Lun|*Mon*	
17 Mar|*Tue*	Louis Vuitton Cup Round Robin 1
18 Mie|*Wed*	
19 Jue|*Thu*	
20 Vie|*Fri*	Día de reserva *Reserve Day*
21 Sáb|*Sat*	Louis Vuitton Cup Round Robin 1
22 Dom|*Sun*	
23 Lun|*Mon*	Día de reserva *Reserve Day*
24 Mar|*Tue*	
25 Mie|*Wed*	
26 Jue|*Thu*	Louis Vuitton Cup Round Robin 2
27 Vie|*Fri*	
28 Sáb|*Sat*	
29 Dom|*Sun*	
30 Lun|*Mon*	

Mayo | *May*

1 Mar|*Tue*	
2 Mie|*Wed*	
3 Jue|*Thu*	Louis Vuitton Cup Round Robin 2
4 Vie|*Fri*	
5 Sáb|*Sat*	
6 Dom|*Sun*	
7 Lun|*Mon*	Día de reserva *Reserve Day*
8 Mar|*Tue*	
9 Mie|*Wed*	
10 Jue|*Thu*	
11 Vie|*Fri*	
12 Sáb|*Sat*	
13 Dom|*Sun*	
14 Lun|*Mon*	
15 Mar|*Tue*	Louis Vuitton Cup Semifinales *Semi Finals*
16 Mie|*Wed*	
17 Jue|*Thu*	
18 Vie|*Fri*	Louis Vuitton Cup Semifinales *Semi Finals*
19 Sáb|*Sat*	
20 Dom|*Sun*	
21 Lun|*Mon*	Día de reserva *Reserve Day*
22 Mar|*Tue*	
23 Mie|*Wed*	Louis Vuitton Cup Semifinales *Semi Finals*
24 Jue|*Thu*	
25 Vie|*Fri*	Día de reserva *Reserve Day*
26 Sáb|*Sat*	
27 Dom|*Sun*	
28 Lun|*Mon*	
29 Mar|*Tue*	
30 Mie|*Wed*	
31 Jue|*Thu*	

* Jornadas posibles de competición de la serie al mejor de nueve.
* *Possible race days of a best of 9 series.*

Competición / Race Schedule

Junio | *June*

1 Vie|*Fri*	
2 Sáb|*Sat*	Louis Vuitton Cup Final
3 Dom|*Sun*	
4 Lun|*Mon*	
5 Mar|*Tue*	Louis Vuitton Cup Final
6 Mie|*Wed*	
7 Jue|*Thu*	Día de reserva *Reserve Day*
8 Vie|*Fri*	☆
9 Sáb|*Sat*	Louis Vuitton Cup Final ☆
10 Dom|*Sun*	☆
11 Lun|*Mon*	☆
12 Mar|*Tue*	Día de reserva *Reserve Day*
13 Mie|*Wed*	
14 Jue|*Thu*	
15 Vie|*Fri*	
16 Sáb|*Sat*	
17 Dom|*Sun*	
18 Lun|*Mon*	
19 Mar|*Tue*	
20 Mie|*Wed*	
21 Jue|*Thu*	
22 Vie|*Fri*	
23 Sáb|*Sat*	32nd America's Cup Match by Louis Vuitton
24 Dom|*Sun*	
25 Lun|*Mon*	
26 Mar|*Tue*	32nd America's Cup Match by Louis Vuitton
27 Mie|*Wed*	
28 Jue|*Thu*	
29 Vie|*Fri*	32nd America's Cup Match by Louis Vuitton
30 Sáb|*Sat*	☆

Julio | *July*

1 Dom|*Sun*	32nd America's Cup Match by Louis Vuitton ☆
2 Lun|*Mon*	
3 Mar|*Tue*	☆
4 Mie|*Wed*	32nd America's Cup Match by Louis Vuitton ☆
5 Jue|*Thu*	
6 Vie|*Fri*	Días de reserva *Reserve Days*
7 Sáb|*Sat*	
8 Dom|*Sun*	
9 Lun|*Mon*	
10 Mar|*Tue*	
11 Mie|*Wed*	
12 Jue|*Thu*	
13 Vie|*Fri*	
14 Sáb|*Sat*	
15 Dom|*Sun*	
16 Lun|*Mon*	
17 Mar|*Tue*	
18 Mie|*Wed*	
19 Jue|*Thu*	
20 Vie|*Fri*	
21 Sáb|*Sat*	
22 Dom|*Sun*	
23 Lun|*Mon*	
24 Mar|*Tue*	
25 Mie|*Wed*	
26 Jue|*Thu*	
27 Vie|*Fri*	
28 Sáb|*Sat*	
29 Dom|*Sun*	
30 Lun|*Mon*	
31 Mar|*Tue*	